BEARS OF THE WORLD™

FAMOUS BEARS

DIANA STAR HELMER

The Rosen Publishing Group's
PowerKids Press™
New York

Published in 1997 by The Rosen Publishing Group, Inc.
29 East 21st Street, New York, NY 10010

First Edition

Book Design: Danielle Primiceri

Photo Credits: Cover by Seth Dinnerman, © PhotoDisc; p. 4 G PhotoDisc; p. 7 © Corbis-Bettmann; p. 8 © Werner Forman Archive/Art Resource; p. 11 © UPI/Corbis-Bettmann; p. 13 © The National Portrait Gallery/Art Resource, p. 19 © U.S. Forest Service.

Photo Illustrations: pp. 12, 15, 16, 20 by Seth Dinnerman.

Helmer, Diana Star, 1962–
    Famous Bears / Diana Star Helmer.
        p.   cm. (Bears of the World)
    Includes index.
    Summary: Examines the significance of bears in our culture and their appearance in religion, symbolism, stories, and astrology.
    ISBN 0-8239-5135-9
    1. Bears—Miscellanea—Juvenile literature. [Bears—Miscellanea.] I. Title. II. Series.
QL737.C27H445 1997
599.78—dc21   96-51023
                                                                                                    CIP
                                                                                                    AC

Manufactured in the United States of America

Table of Contents

Bears, Bears, Bears

People have been telling stories about bears for hundreds of years. Today, we tell stories about Baloo the Bear, Br'er Bear, Little Bear, the Berenstein Bears, Care Bears, SuperTed, and others. We have surrounded ourselves with bears. Why?

Bears are sort of like people. They sit and stand, like people do. They use their paws like hands. Bears eat vegetables, meats, and sweets. They teach and care for their young. Goldilocks wanted to know more about the three bears. We want to learn more about bears, too. What famous bears do you know?

◀ *People have been interested in bears for hundreds of years.*

Bears in the Sky

In the night sky, one star stays still as other stars circle around it. That one, still star is called the Pole Star. The Pole Star and the other stars nearby make **constellations** (kon-stel-AY-shunz), or pictures, in the sky. Hundreds of years ago, two of these pictures were given the same name by different people all over the world: Great Bear and Little Bear.

How did all those people see the same two pictures? And why did they name those pictures the same names?

Long ago, bears were at the center of many **religions** (ree-LIH-juhnz). That's probably why so many different people saw bears in the center of the sky.

Another name for the Great Bear ▶
constellation is Ursa Major.

Bear Spirits

Religions help people not to be afraid of what they don't know. For example, no one really knows what death is like. But Native American, **Hindu** (HIN-doo), and **Christian** (KRIS-chen) religions have all used the way bears **hibernate** (HY-ber-nayt) to teach people about death.

Each year, bears make dens. They go into the dens to hibernate. Bears sleep through the winter, as if they were not alive. But during the winter, mother bears give birth to bear cubs. In the spring, the bears and their cubs come out of their dens. Many religions teach that life goes on after death, like the bears waking up with their cubs when winter is over.

◄ *Many Native American tribes use bears to stand for different things. This bear carving stands for the Brown Bear group of Tlingit Indians. The Tlingit live in Alaska.*

Bear's Day

Long ago in Europe, people began to **celebrate** (SEL-uh-brayt) Bear's Day. On February 2, six weeks after the longest night of winter, people hoped that the bear had lost its shadow. Why?

Because people believed that shadows belonged to living things. If a bear saw its shadow on Bear's Day, the bear had not left its old life. People believed that winter would last until the bear woke from its hibernation without a shadow. A bear with no shadow brought new life, or spring. People in parts of Poland, Austria, and Hungary still celebrate Bear's Day.

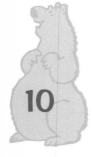

Long ago, many people believed that bears brought spring with them when they awoke from their long winter's sleep. ▶

Tender-Hearted Teddy

Almost everyone likes teddy bears. But did you know that teddy bears earned their name from former U.S. President Teddy Roosevelt?

Roosevelt liked to hunt. One day in 1902, when he was hunting, he had the chance to shoot a bear cub. But he wouldn't shoot it. Lots of people thought that was funny. Newspapers printed a cartoon of what happened. Shop owner Morris Michtom put the cartoon in his store window, next to a toy bear. So many people wanted one of "Teddy's Bears," that Michtom started a toy company that made teddy bears. Other toy makers around the world started making teddy bears, too.

Former President Teddy Roosevelt

◀ *Children all over the world enjoy teddy bears today.*

Rupert Bear

Rupert Bear lives in Nutwood, a magical place where the past and present meet. But most people know of Rupert from London's *Daily Express* newspaper. Rupert is the longest-running comic strip **character** (KAYR-ek-ter) in the world. The first comic strip about him was printed on November 8, 1920. And it kept going, even during World War II, when the *Express* was only one page. Rupert was on that one page, cheering people up. By the time Rupert was 75 years old, he had a fan club, a television show, and, of course, his comic strip.

Rupert Bear is even on the Internet! ▶

Winnie-the-Pooh

Most people have heard of the bear Winnie-the-Pooh. But did you know that there really was a boy named Christopher Robin? And he really had a teddy bear he named Winnie-the-Pooh. Christopher Robin's father, A. A. Milne, wrote a book about them in 1926. The book was called *Winnie-the-Pooh*.

Milne usually wrote stories for grown-ups. He wasn't sure if he liked being **famous** (FAY-mus) for a children's story. But grown-ups love Winnie-the-Pooh, too. Other adults have written grown-up books about what they learned from Pooh. Although Pooh called himself "a bear of little brain," many people think Pooh's heart was very wise.

◀ *So many people like Winnie-the-Pooh that he appears on everything from cups to notebooks to sweatshirts.*

Smokey Bear

Smokey Bear wasn't a real bear—at first. Smokey started as a **symbol** (SIM-buhl) to remind people to be careful with fire. The U.S. Forest Service created Smokey in 1944 to help protect forests and animals.

Then, in 1950, a fire burned New Mexico's Lincoln National Forest. A bear cub was found in a burned tree. Newspapers called him "Smokey." When the cub was well enough, he went to the National Zoo in Washington, DC. Millions of people visited "Smokey."

Today, people around the world know Smokey's message: "Remember, only you can prevent forest fires."

Smokey Bear's familiar face helps us ▶
remember to be careful with fire.

SMOKEY'S A-B-C's

Always break matches in two!

Be sure fires are out-cold!

Crush all smokes dead!

Paddington

In this series:
Paddington's ABC
Paddington's 123
Paddington's Colors
Paddington's Opposites

Paddington's ABC

by Michael Bond
illustrated by John Lobban

Paddington Bear

One Christmas Eve, a man named Michael Bond bought a teddy bear near the Paddington train station in London, England. And in 1958, Bond wrote the book, *A Bear Called Paddington*.

In the book, the Brown family finds a real, talking bear at Paddington Station. He is from "Darkest Peru," where **Andean** (AN-dee-un) bears live. Paddington moves into the Browns' home in London. Life with humans can be difficult, but Paddington never gives up.

Paddington has starred in many funny books and plays. He's had several television series and is known all over the world.

◀ *You may have read books about Paddington Bear, too.*

Caring About Bears

Hundreds of years ago, people told stories about bears who were strong and gentle. Those bears lived together with people in the forest. They helped people by providing them with food and shelter.

In the 1800s, bear stories changed. In America, **folk figures** (fohk FIG-yerz), such as Daniel Boone, fought with bears and often killed them.

Today, bear stories are often about teddy bears. Teddy bears need people to take care of them. Maybe we tell these stories because we know we must care for all bears. Bears need us. And our stories show that we need bears, too.

Glossary

Andean (AN-dee-un) From the Andes Mountains of South America.

celebrate (SEL-uh-brayt) To enjoy a special time in honor of something.

character (KAYR-ek-ter) A personality in a book, play, movie, television show, or radio show.

Christian (KRIS-chen) A religion that teaches the ideas of Jesus Christ.

constellation (kon-stel-AY-shun) A group of stars that makes a picture.

famous (FAY-mus) Very well-known.

folk figures (fohk FIG-yerz) People about whom stories are often told.

hibernate (HY-ber-nayt) To sleep through the winter without eating.

Hindu (HIN-doo) A religion that started in India.

religion (ree-LIH-juhn) Ideas about the universe and about how people should act that a group of people agree on and follow.

symbol (SIM-buhl) An image or a picture that stands for something else.

23

Index